RODEO
PUP

To Jeffrey and Carrie,
with thanks to the real Rodeo Pup.

A FIREFLY BOOK

Copyright © 1998 Lisa Rotenberg

Parents please note: While dogs do require regular dental care,
actual flossing of dog teeth is not necessary.

Cataloguing in Publication Data

Rotenberg, Lisa
Rodeo pup

ISBN 1-55209-245-3

I. Title.

PS8585.084345R62 1998a   jC813'.54   C98-930180-X
PZ7.R67Ro 1998

Published in the United States in 1998
by Firefly Books (U.S.) Inc.
P.O. Box 1338, Ellicott Station
Buffalo, New York, USA
14205

Text and cover design by Lisa Rotenberg
Printed and bound in Canada

RODEO PUP

WORDS AND PICTURES BY LISA ROTENBERG

FIREFLY BOOKS

My dog
Rodeo Pup
is much
smarter
than he
looks.

He can
turn
almost
any day
into an
adventure.

It was
picture-
taking day.

When I got up,
I put on
my best
skirt and
matching
fishnet
tights.

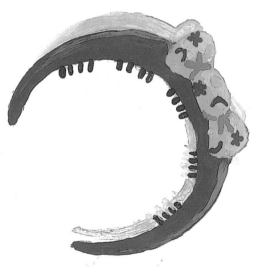

WHEN IT COMES TO FISHNET TIGHTS, THE BRIGHTER THE BETTER.

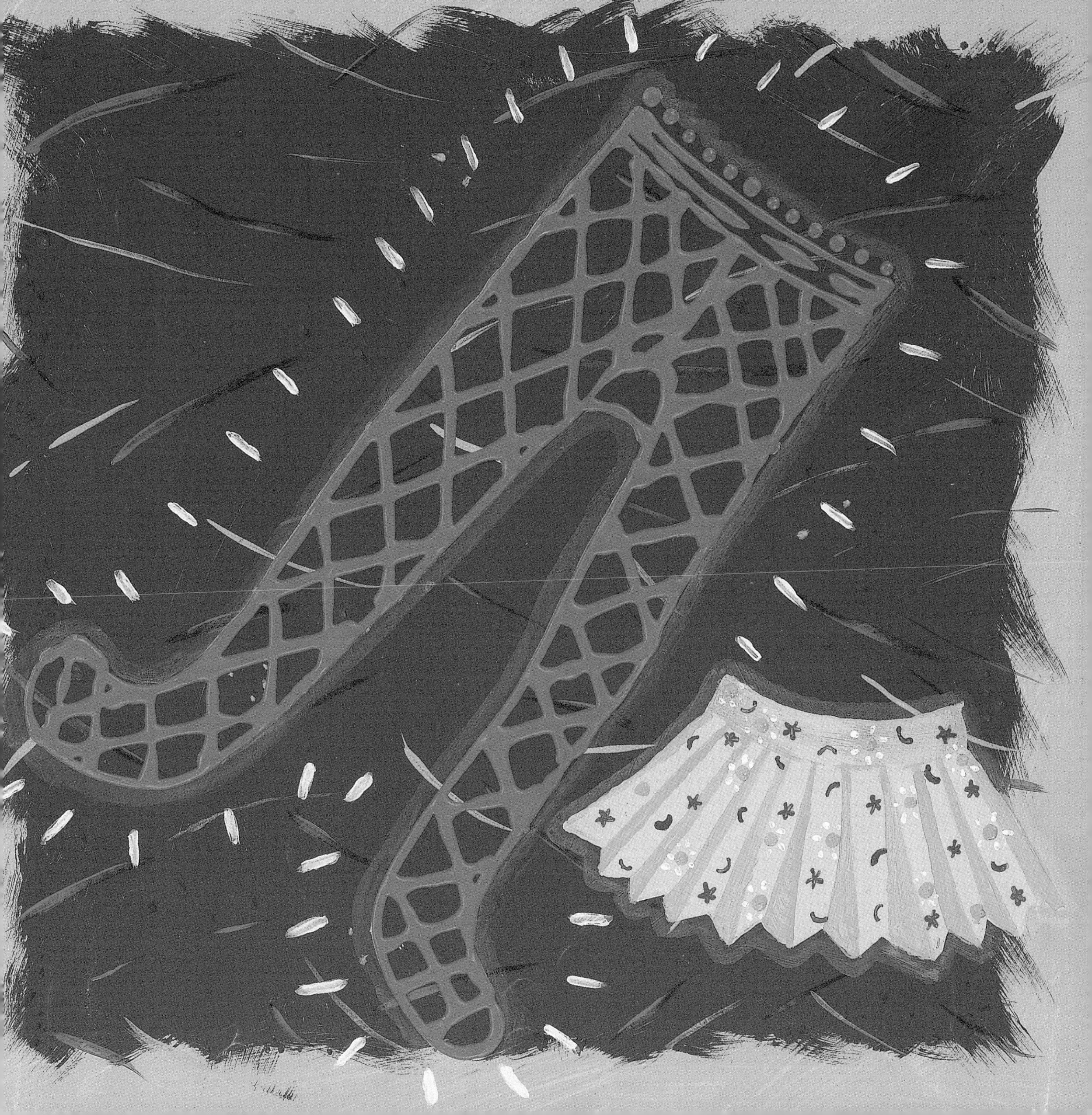

At breakfast,
Rodeo Pup begged
me to get
his Dino-Chew
bone from his
crate (where he sleeps).

I crawled into
that crate to fetch it.

Rodeo Pup ate
my toast.

A DOG'S CRATE, BIG OR SMALL, IS HIS CASTLE.

HOME
SWEET
CRATE

RODEO PUP
IS
OUT

R P

R P

While I was
on my way to
school,
Rodeo Pup
escaped
from our
backyard to
see where
I was going
in such
fancy
clothes.

A DOG'S YARD MUST BE SECURE TO KEEP HIM SAFE FROM HARM.

Suddenly,
Rodeo Pup
grabbed
my fishnet
tights with
his teeth
(he would
never, ever
hurt me)
and unraveled
them as he ran
off towards
the school yard.

OME DOGS WILL CHEW ON ANYTHING, EVEN IF IT'S NOT GOOD FOR THEM.

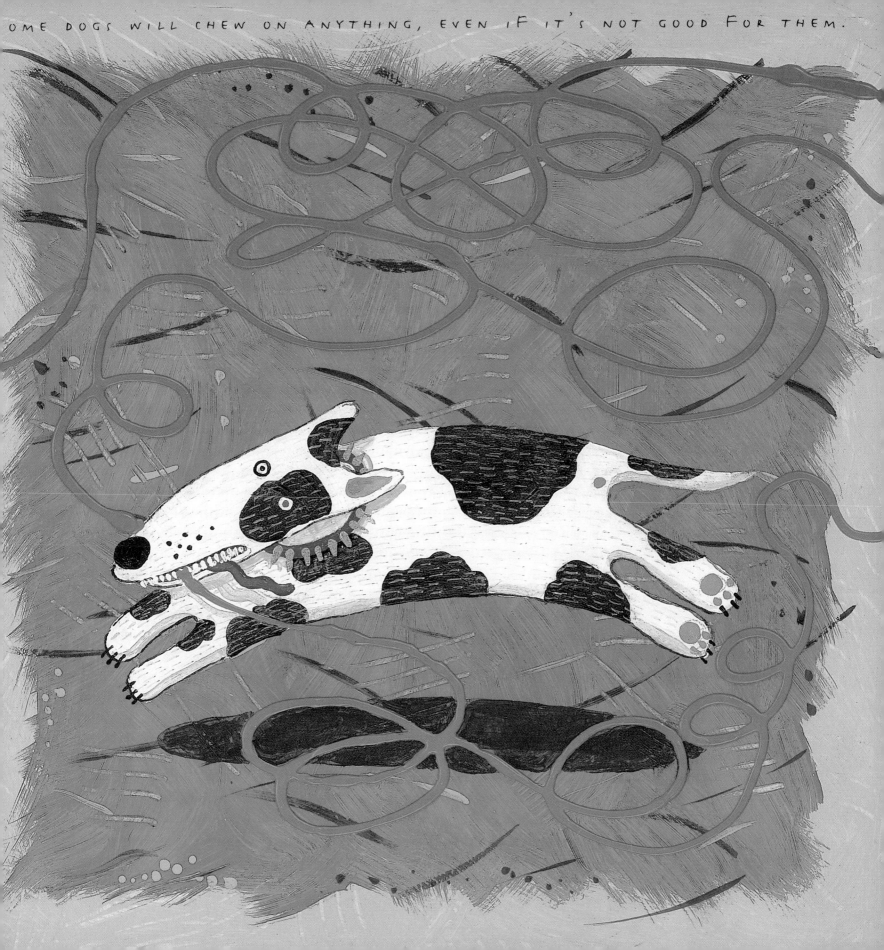

Later,
in the school's office,
my teacher
comforted me.

Rodeo Pup
had to sit
very still
and be on
his best
behavior.

TELL YOUR DOG WHEN HE IS BAD. HE'LL KNOW BETTER NEXT TIME.

Mother
soon arrived
with new
fishnet tights and
to see if I
was all right.

She asked
Rodeo Pup,
"Well, what
do you have
to say for
yourself?"

SOMETIMES EVEN A GOOD DOG CAN GET INTO TROUBLE.

Mother
then
took
Rodeo Pup
home
on his
leash.

WALKING YOUR DOG ON A LEASH WILL SHOW HIM WHO'S THE BOSS.

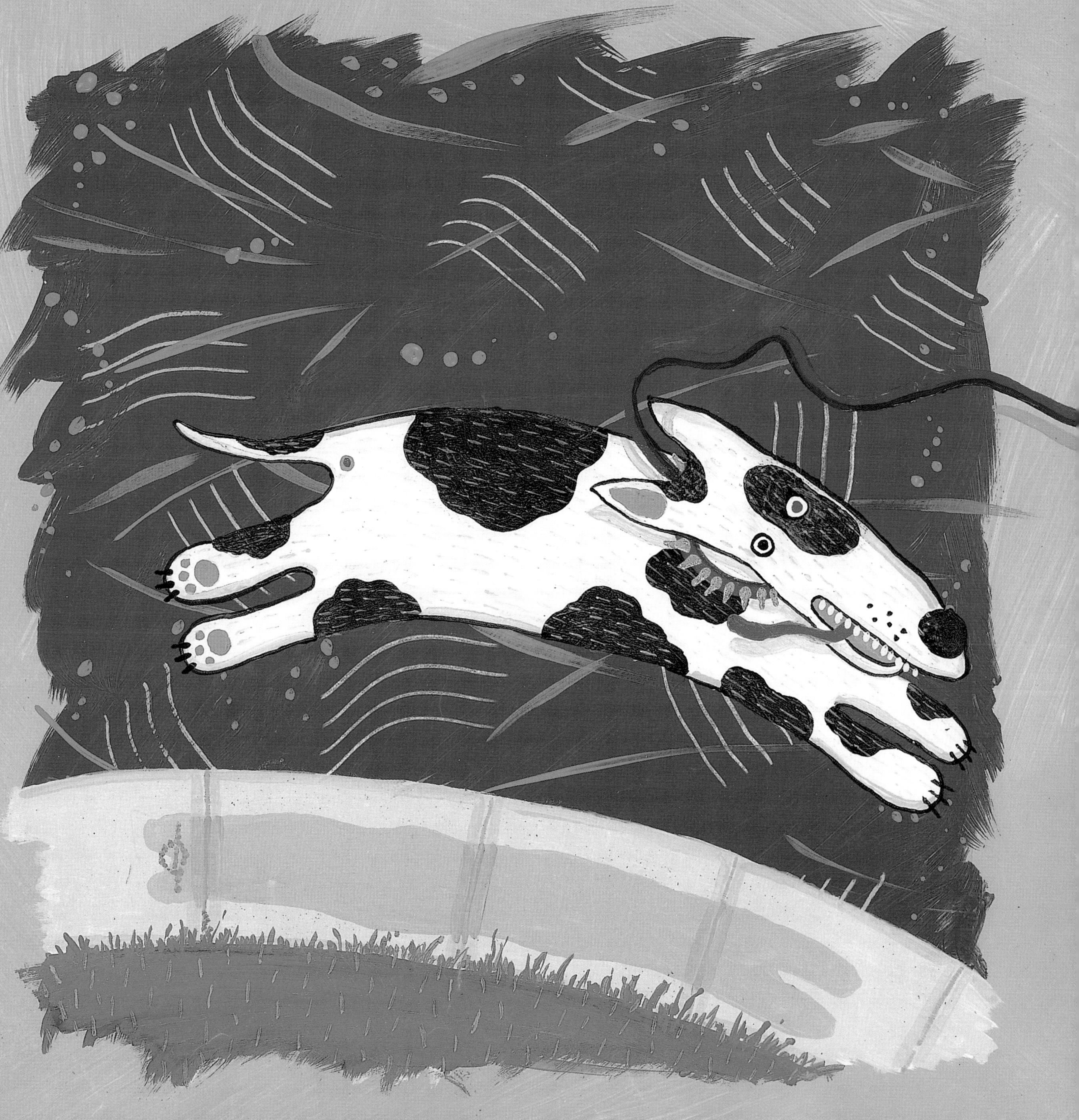

After school,
Rodeo Pup
greeted me and
rolled over on
his back
(which means
"I'm sorry"
in dog talk).

Then he took a
L-O-N-G
piece of string
from behind
the couch.

RODEO PUP ISN'T ALLOWED ON THE COUCH.

Rodeo Pup
took the
string
and flossed
his teeth.

I told
you
he's
smart.

YOU KNOW, DOGS NEED TO TAKE CARE OF THEIR TEETH LIKE WE DO.

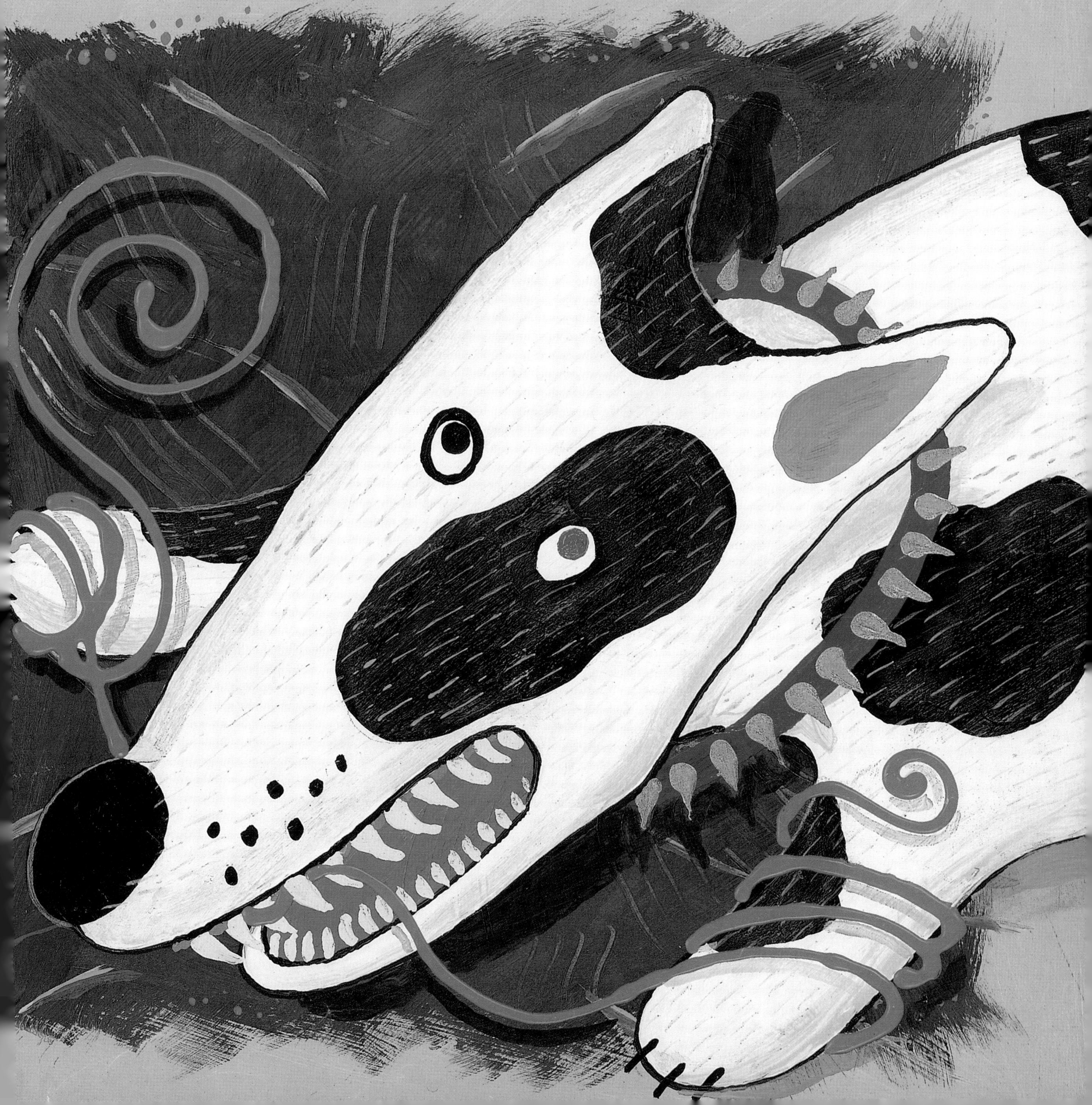

Well.

Father was amazed.

Mother was speechless.

My brother took a picture.

RODEO PUP JUST LOVES POSING FOR PICTURES!

The
very
next
day,
Rodeo Pup's
picture
was in
the
newspaper.

SEEING OUR DOG'S PICTURE IN THE PAPER WAS A DREAM COME TRUE.

And
now,
children
from
all over
send
Rodeo Pup
fan mail!

AIR MAIL
PAR AVION

Rodeo Pup
310

RUSH!

RODEO PUP LOVES CARDS AND LETTERS, BUT E-MAIL IS HIS FAVORITE.

Rodeo Pup
would
like to hear
from you!

You can
visit his
website at
http://www.rodeopup.com
and if you send an e-mail,
he'll write back.

He really
is one smart dog!

WITHDRAWN 1999